THE FALLEN RING

—·—

KEY DAWKINS

CONTENTS

Our intentions may be very good, but, because
the intelligence is limited, the action may turn
out to be a mistake – a mistake, but not nec-
essarily a sin, for sin comes out of a wrong
intention.

E. Stanley Jones

CHAPTER 1

'Are you sure you don't want to come over, James?' asked Simon Jones as he stopped walking. He turned towards his friend and looked at him squarely.

Avoiding Simon's gaze, James Huang fixed his eyes on the concrete below their feet. He hesitated before answering. 'Yeah, I'm sure. I, uh, have things that I need to do when I get back.'

Sensing his friend's uneasiness, Simon placed a firm hand on James's shoulder. 'Look, I know things aren't great at home, but I want you to know that I'm here for you. We've been friends so long that I now consider you a brother. And, as always, my door is open to you … should you feel you want to talk.'

James looked up with a melancholic smile and nodded softly. 'Thank you, Simon. It really means a lot.' He held Simon's gaze for a moment.

'It's what we do,' said Simon, smiling as he nodded ahead. 'Better get going, our science project won't do itself.'

Walking side by side, the teenagers continued on their way home through their local neighbourhood. The boys didn't live far from one another, yet it sometimes felt as if they lived miles apart. Simon lived within the middle-class area of the city, whereas James lived closer to the working-class area. In spite of this, the teenagers were inseparable. At seventeen years of age, they had a close friendship, one that had begun in their early days of secondary school.

On reaching James's house, the boys said their goodbyes and parted ways for the afternoon, but Simon hung back, watching his friend from a short distance away. He felt a loyal obligation to watch over his friend, as he had done many times before. He had only heard James's account of what his life was like at home; he had never seen it for himself. Concealed behind a few trees, he watched James walk up to the door of his small house on the corner of the street. James rapped on the front door and stood patiently outside, waiting for someone to let him in.

After a slow minute or so, the door swung open and a man came into view. It was James's father: a tall, skinny man with a twisted scowl and a beer bottle in his hand. James's mouth was moving but could not quite make out what he was saying. By the expression on his face and the gestures he was making, it looked as though he was desperately trying to explain something, but with little success. Before he had finished, James's father shouted something unintelligible at his son before grabbing him by the shirt collar and yanking him into the house. The thunderous slam of the door ricocheted across the street. He shrank back into the foliage, pushing his back up against the tree behind him.

Simon's eyes widened, his heart pounding out of his chest. No wonder James had never invited him to his house in all the years he had known him. He could now understand his anxiety and depressed outlook on life. The sadness in James's eyes was all too apparent. All it took was one glimpse for a grim picture of his friend's life to come together. Deep down, Simon could feel a burning rage building within him: a deep-seated anger at seeing his close friend bullied and hurt. It was enough that James had been picked on during secondary school, but this was something else. This was abuse: a cruel and protracted experience that no one deserved. Unfortunately, he knew, deep down, there was nothing he could do. If James wanted a way out, he would have told him – but he hadn't. The best he could do right now was watch and listen and offer his friend as much consoling comfort as he could muster.

Chapter 2

Simon stared towards the front of the classroom, his physical body in attendance, but his mind wandering elsewhere. What he had witnessed yesterday would not fade from his memory. The shocking images and sounds had plagued his mind the previous night as he stared up at his ceiling, his mind vacant of everything else save for his friend's predicament. How he hadn't realised the magnitude of the situation earlier, he didn't know. But now that he had, the disturbing images were unrelenting. James's glum face passed before his eyes over and over again on constant replay. He wished he could do more for his dear friend, to truly help him in some way.

He turned towards the window near his desk, his mind still roving. Like the clouds that had once been white but were now grey and heavy, he felt his mood sour. As he continued to stare into the darkened and overcast sky, something caught his eye: a small, silvery object that twinkled as it fell past the window. It was almost unnoticeable. His eyes followed the object until it quickly disappeared from view, finding a resting place somewhere below.

'You are paying attention, aren't you, Simon?' came the voice of Arthur Mansfield, Simon's teacher.

Startled out of his trance, he turned back to the front of the classroom, his eyes meeting Mr Mansfield's. 'Yes, of course. My apologies, sir.'

Mr Mansfield nodded towards Simon before resuming his lesson on themes within English literature. As he droned on, Simon swiftly relapsed back into his trance, his mind once again wandering elsewhere. Mr Mansfield's voice gradually receded, giving way to his piqued curiosity. What was that silver object? Where did it come from?

———

After class Simon wandered towards the landing site of the silver object – or at least where he thought it might have landed. He conducted a quick inspection of the grounds below the classroom window, his fingers sifting through the wet grass as he looked for his quarry. A twinkle in a patch of grass to his right caught his eye. Quickly pushing aside the grass, he uncovered a small, shiny, circular object nestled amongst the strands.

It was a metallic ring.

Looking about himself, he carefully picked up the ring and brought it up to his eyes for a better look. Upon closer examination, there looked to be some sort of runes engraved around the inner rim. They didn't mean anything to him, yet there was something alluring about them, something cryptic and intriguing. A faint glow emanated from them, a soft but vibrant purple light that captivated him. It was almost enchanting. Holding the ring between his index finger and thumb, he felt a subtle wave of anomalous energy surge through and across his body, instantly lifting his mood and elevating his senses. He felt refreshed and energised.

As the glowing runes slowly faded, he felt himself return to normal. What on earth had just happened? Whatever it was, it felt supernatural; he had never felt this way before. He stared at the ring. Where had it come from? How did it get here? Who did it belong to? As he continued to gaze at the strange silver ring, the thought of slipping it onto his index finger crossed his mind. The thought then became an unconscious action as he slowly raised his hand and began to slide the ring onto his finger. Just then, his eyes caught the time displayed on his watch. It was twenty past one in the afternoon. He would be late for his next class if he didn't leave now. Scooping the ring into a clenched hand, he thrust the ring into his jeans pocket and looked around the campus grounds. No one was paying much attention as most of the students were heading back to class. He joined the communal march back to lessons, deep in thought. What had just happened to him? Was it the ring? How was that possible? Regardless of the answers, he knew one thing for sure.

The ring was his now.

———

James couldn't help but feel that Simon was a being bit more distant than usual. It was as though something else was occupying his mind, but he couldn't put his finger on it.

'It doesn't matter what I do. He's always having a go at me for something or the other. It's worse when he's drunk. Then there's no stopping him. That's why my mum's always out working, while I face the brunt of it. I hate that we have to live with it, but I don't know what to do. I don't want to upset my mum or do something that I might regret, if you know what I mean.'

'I know, James. I know,' said Simon looking away, his fingers running over the ring in his pocket. 'I wish you weren't going through what you're going through. I can only imagine.'

The teenagers walked on in silence for the rest of the way, each consumed in their own thoughts until they reached James's neighbourhood.

'Well, here I am,' said James, failing an attempt at a smile.

Simon looked at the pained expression of his friend and sighed. 'You know, you don't deserve this, James. No one does. If only you could live with me and my family. Things would be so different for you then. We would always be together, as friends. As brothers.'

James turned away with a look of resignation. 'If only. The imagination is a wonderful thing.'

Simon placed a hand on his friend's shoulder. 'One day, things are going to change for you, and only for the better. Trust me.'

'Maybe,' said James in a quiet voice. It was the only word he could think of saying in response. He hoped his friend was right, but he didn't place much trust in hopes.

———

The boys said their goodbyes and parted ways as normal. Once again, Simon hung back and watched James approach his house on the corner of the street. He paused outside the front door, his head hanging low. With a sigh, he withdrew a key from his pocket and let himself in.

Simon exhaled loudly, unaware he had been holding his breath. He hadn't wanted to see his friend suffer as he had the day before. Despite that, he knew he was suffering internally every day, and that his pain was the worst of all: the feeling of hopelessness. He waited for a few moments longer, reflecting on his friend's situation. As he did, he felt a warm sensation in his pocket – the silver ring.

Slipping his hand into his pocket, he retrieved the ring. The runes were glowing the vibrant purple he had seen earlier. But they were much brighter than before and the ring was radiating an intense warmth. Once again, he found himself drawn towards the ring, mesmerised by its mysterious nature and fascinating glow. He began to slip it onto his finger.

A car horn sounded, snapping him out of his trance and back to reality. He glanced up to see two cars pass along the narrow road and out of the neighbourhood. He returned his gaze to the ring in his palm. The runes had stopped glowing and the warmth had ceased.

He pocketed the ring once again and turned on his heel.

Chapter 3

After dinner that evening, Simon rushed back up to his bedroom, his mind taken with one thing: the silver ring. Desiring peace and quiet, he had managed to wait until nightfall to take a closer look. He didn't want to involve his parents or sister just yet. Sitting at his wooden desk opposite his bed, he held the ring between his index finger and thumb, turning it over. Had he missed anything earlier in the day? Perhaps a tiny detail that would reveal more about the peculiar ring. To his dismay, however, nothing new unveiled itself. All he could see were the strange runes around the inner rim. It was puzzling. Where had the ring come from? Why was it warm and how did it glow? Did it belong to someone? The questions circulated around the forefront of his mind. He suspected there was more to the ring than met the eye. Having experienced two inexplicable events already, would there be a third?

Then, the thought that had occurred to him earlier returned: *try it on.*

He turned the ring between his fingers once more, the thought growing more tempting with each passing second. He tried to resist the enticing pull of the ring but found that he was unable. Like a magnet, he was drawn to its alluring force. Raising his right hand, he carefully slipped the silver ring onto his middle finger, pushing it up as far as it would go, and waited for a reaction.

At first, nothing seemed to happen. But then the runes began to glow a brilliant and vibrant purple and a warmth spread through the metal band. Alarmed, he tried to remove the ring, but his arm would not budge; he had lost control of his body. A surge of energy washed over him, replenishing him, making him feel stronger, and a current of power filled his veins, spreading like wildfire across his body. Engulfed in a force so powerful and unknown, he began to lose consciousness, his world spinning and growing dark all around him. He had never felt such a heavy burden before, the coursing energy travelling up to his head, spreading to the corners of his mind. It was as though something had invaded him. In his mind's eye his memories and thoughts and his feelings and emotions played out before him, clearer than ever.

Overtaken by the unknown foreign force, he collapsed, powerless to resist.

Covered from head to toe in a dark purple, metallic-like liquid that sheened in the moonlight, Simon barely recognised himself. With luminous purple eyes staring back at him in the mirror, he shuddered. What was all this? What was going on? What had he done? As multiple questions raced across his mind, he felt his adrenaline spike: flight or fight was kicking in. He was frightened, alarmed and somehow excited.

Breathing deeply, he peered into the mirror and felt his heartbeat slow. His eyes grew wider at the sight of his new form: muscles rippling in the light and shadow; he felt immensely strong, fast and full of vigour. His thoughts returned to the silver ring. It must have been the cause. He had experienced similar sensations when he first held the ring. Unlike before, however, this felt different – this felt permanent. Or at least, he felt it could be.

As he gazed at his reflection, a voice floated up from somewhere deep within: *It's all yours. Just imagine the possibilities … What you can do … What we can do … What we can achieve.*

Where was it coming from? He didn't know, and he didn't care. He felt fantastic and that's all that mattered. He felt unstoppable.

The whispering voice came again. *If we join together, you shall be bestowed with knowledge that you could never fathom. You shall see that which you have never seen. You shall attain that of which you could only dream. Together we shall achieve something far bigger and grander than ourselves.*

Subconsciously, Simon could feel himself agreeing. It was almost nourishing, the energy that was coursing through his body, through his muscles, through his veins. Simon thought the words that he wanted to say, and as though in immediate response, a flurry of cryptic glyphs, images and text flashed before him. Initially, he didn't know what he was seeing or what was happening, but then it became clearer. He was being merged with the force within. A sense of calm washed over him. It felt as though he had been reborn; only bigger, stronger and much more than he ever thought possible.

Feeling refreshed and full of purpose, he gathered his thoughts, his recent memories flooding back in. One stuck out amongst the rest: his dear friend James. He recalled his situation, his pain and his sorrow. He also remembered the source. A scorching rage far greater than before boiled within his chest. He knew what had to be done and he would see to it that it was taken care of.

What are you waiting for?

He approached his window and raised the sash. The cool night breeze rushed in across his face. Clouds were brewing and rain was not far away, the dark sky bristling with the threat of thunder.

Tonight, retribution was in the air.

F ootsteps thundered throughout the house long before they reached his cramped room. When the door burst open, he knew all too well what to expect.

'You think you can just laze around whenever you want? What did I tell you about doing what you're told?' shouted James's father. 'Maybe it's not getting through to you. Maybe I need to get more physical. Then you'll learn!'

'No, no, I remember what you said. I didn't forget. I was just doing my homework. I promise I'll do the chores. Just please don't … Give me another chance, I beg you.' James cowered on the bed.

'You've been given enough chances. I don't buy you just *doing your homework*. I saw you with that friend of yours … walking home at your own pace.' James's father strode into the room. 'You think you can lie to me? You dare lie to me?'

James raised his hands in protest. He was about to utter something in response but was cut off.

'I know what you're *going* to do. You're *going* to start with your filthy mess of a room.' He threw his fist down on James's bed, knocking his books and equipment off the blanket and toppling them to the floor.

James looked down at his scattered possessions, his emotions ablaze. He wanted to say something, but his throat felt choked.

'Clean up this crap now or else! Do you understand me?' said James's father. He stiffened and turned to exit the bedroom.

'This is why things are the way they are! This is why Mum is rarely ever here! You and your controlling—' James felt the rough, bony hands of his father whip against his cheek. Falling backwards, he landed hard on his side.

James's father stepped closer to his son, bringing his face down to his. 'If you ever dare mention your mother again, you'll have more than just a bruise. Is that clear? Don't ever speak to me like that again, you disappointing fool.'

James's nose wrinkled at the smell of stale alcohol on his father's breath.

'Clean your mess up,' barked James's father, withdrawing from the room and slamming the door on his way out.

Lying on the cold bedroom floor, James curled himself into a foetal position. Weak, vulnerable and alone, it was a similar routine every day, and he felt progressively worse with each passing second. He wanted to scream. To shout. But he knew he couldn't and wouldn't – not unless he wanted another beating.

Hugging his knees tightly, he prayed for a way out, for some reprieve, for some consolation. But he knew it was a long shot.

Who would help him? And why now?

CHAPTER 4

S itting on the rear porch steps in the garden, James's father took a swig from his bottle of liquor and watched the rainfall. Feeling the bitter burn trickle down his throat, he felt a sense of superiority. He enjoyed beating down on people, making them feel small and powerless. It made him feel strong and imposing. It was the look in people's eyes when they knew they were helpless to do anything. When they had no other option but to obey him. It was one of the few things he adored. It made him feel alive. It was also one of the few things that took his mind off his problems.

Ever since he had made that reckless decision so many years ago, he had felt himself diminish day by day. The ever-looming debt had seemingly bound him for the rest of his life. Had he not made that fateful choice, perhaps his life might have been different. But it meant nothing now. His life was already over and there was only one way out: death. Either that, or something possibly worse. The mafia boss he owed money to was not someone to cross. He was ruthless and always extracted payment – one way or another. He had tried to escape once, but it had ended terribly. For three days, he had been kept in an underground pit after being beaten badly. And for days he had wept silently, feeling every bit as vulnerable and hopeless as the people he had intimidated and leaned on during his lifetime.

He hadn't intended to have a child, but as often happens life had other ideas. He'd met James's mother in his thirties during a job for his boss. Their relationship had never been great, but for one reason or another she had stayed. Whether it was for the child or not, he didn't care. They were insignificant to him in the grand scheme of things. The unpaid debt consumed his every waking second. If he could repay it, maybe he could reclaim some shred of his life back. But then again, no one was ever really free of Marcus Crawford. Once you were in his debt, you were never truly free. He had seen Crawford make examples of some of his victims, and he quivered at the prospect of becoming the next in line.

Taking a final swig from his now empty whisky bottle, he got to his feet and stretched his legs. With a yawn, he turned towards the neglected house and made his way towards the steps. A scratching sound stopped him in his tracks. Craning his neck, he listened to his surroundings. Had it been a fox? Could it have been the neighbourhood cats? A few moments of silence passed, broken only by the light patter of rainfall and the distant grumble of thunder. Shaking his head in dismissal, he started up the steps. But before he could make it to the back door, the distinct sound pierced the night air once again. Only this time, it sounded closer. James's father swung his head around, his eyes straining into the darkness. Despite the liquor, he could feel his heartbeat begin to race. The thought of a visit from Crawford's men made him shudder. He had made the last payment as per the arranged schedule. What would bring them to him now? He pushed the dreadful thought aside. It couldn't be them; this wasn't their style.

Seeing nothing but drizzly rainfall, he took a final glance around before breathing a sigh of relief. Must have been an animal. As he turned back towards the house, his heart caught in his throat. Towering before him was a dark humanoid figure. In the scant light, he could make out the metallic sheen of its smooth skin. Its breathing was steady, and its eyes were bright, unwavering and trained on him. Dropping to his knees, James's father started to shake uncontrollably. Like prey, he cowered in front of the predator. Before he had time to react, the dark figure lashed out at him.

The wind was knocked from his lungs as he was thrown backwards, crashing into the old iron fence at the back of the garden. There was a sickening crack as he tumbled over, face planting into the wet dirt. Barely conscious, he groaned in agony as pain shot up from his lower back. Something was injured if not broken. Managing to tilt his head upward, he watched in horror as the dark figure descended the steps onto the patches of grass. It was tall, muscular and menacing. Most terrifying of all, its luminous purple eyes never left his, fixing him with a steely stare, it's eyes boring into his. He flailed his arms in a desperate effort to crawl away, but it was no use. His body was too bruised and beaten. He wouldn't be going anywhere anytime soon. The dark figure, now upon him, knelt down, bringing its face down to his, surveying its victim.

'Please, don't …' croaked James's father, now at the mercy of the strange life form.

The dark figure, as though assessing his words, narrowed its eyes. Then, in a deep and gravelly voice, it spoke: 'You are undeserving of mercy, and so shall receive none.'

Stunned by the merciless words, he gasped in horror as the dark figure extended its muscular hands and clasped them over his face, darkness seeping into the corners of his brain as consciousness abandoned him.

Chapter 5

'Don't you understand what I'm saying? My father has been hospitalised … the condition I found him in this morning … bruised and battered … he was hardly breathing. It was like someone had brutalised him and left him for dead,' said James in a desperate voice.

Unable to understand James's feelings of concern, Simon shot his friend a quizzical look. How did he do it? How could he feel so empathetic towards his father? Especially after everything he had done. How could he feel even one shred of remorse? Why did he care? Shouldn't he be feeling liberated, free from that tyrant? 'You're right. I don't understand. I thought you hated him. After everything you've told me, all the stories, all the pain, why are you so concerned about him? Why do you feel so strongly? Why do you even care?'

James blinked, taken aback by his friend's response. 'What do you mean why do I care? He's my father. He's never acted like it and it never felt like it. But I still care about him. He may have caused my mother and I much grief, but he's still my father. Still … still a parent.'

Seeing his friend distraught over his abusive father, a man who wasn't worth a penny, Simon couldn't help but feel contempt. How ungrateful of James to not see the good turn of events. The man who had blighted his life now removed, and he still didn't see the light? How emotionally weak could he be? To not appreciate the vengeance that had been exacted by a Samaritan who had responded to his plea for help. 'I don't believe this. That bastard finally gets what he deserves, and you're feeling sorry for him. Tell me what I'm missing here.'

'You want to know what you're missing here? You don't understand my life and never will. To live in such conditions … to feel alienated and alone. To have no real support,' said James, pursing his lips. 'My father may have done a lot of bad things, but he's still family. He's one of the few things I've got left.'

Hearing his friend's words, Simon could feel his rage returning. He wanted to shout at James. To shake him to his senses. But deep down, something felt wrong. Why was he getting so worked up? Sure, his alter ego was responsible for putting James's father in critical condition, but James didn't know that. And judging by his reaction, it should stay that way too. Taking a deep breath, Simon calmed his nerves. He was coming across too strong, almost too proud of what he had done. 'I'm sorry, James. I … I don't know what came over me.'

'I don't either,' said James. He held Simon's gaze and shook his head. 'Look, I should really be checking on my mum. See if she's okay and all. Maybe we can talk later.'

Nodding his agreement, Simon turned away from his friend's house. It wasn't supposed to be this way. When he had arrived earlier, he had caught sight of the ambulance and James's father being wheeled in on a stretcher. Seeing the man in such a condition had brought him a sense of relief – at least at first. Knowing that he had freed his friend from an abusive tyrant, he had slept easier after the incident. But as he put more space between himself and his friend's neighbourhood, he began to feel something else. Remorse? Regret? No, it couldn't be. What he had done was right. It had to have been. He couldn't watch his friend suffer anymore. He had done what any good friend would have done: he had helped.

Reflecting on his actions, he subconsciously stroked the silver ring on his middle finger. As he rubbed its smooth rim, feeling the warmth emanate out of it, the whispering voice resurfaced. *Why do you doubt? Didn't we do what was right? What was necessary? Without our intervention, your friend would continue to suffer, wouldn't he?*

Finding few grounds to object, he couldn't help but agree. He had done what had needed to be done. He had put an end to his friend's suffering, and that's all that mattered. Regardless of whether James could appreciate it or not, he had been freed. The voice was right, and in time James would come to see that. In time, everyone would.

CHAPTER 6

Marcus Crawford was a hard as nails monster of a man. Tall and stocky in build, he had an air of grandiosity about him. From his expensive dark suit to his polished brown shoes, he was every bit as prideful as his ego would allow. Growing up in an impoverished family in his youth, Marcus had made it his mission to rise above the ranks. He had told everyone who would listen that one day he would become the boss, and when that day came, everyone who had doubted him would suffer the consequences.

He had been pitiless in his ascent to power and had no intention of relenting. From narcotics to weapons to gambling, he had made his mark on London's unforgiving underworld. His name was known to many, and its mere mention made even the most hardened criminals shiver. When it came to collecting his debts, he would ensure he received his dues. He spared none and made examples of those who crossed or tested him. Marcus would not tolerate an attempt at usurpation, and if it was discovered that one of his men showed even the slightest inclination, they would end up wishing they were dead.

'It has come to my attention that you have been found guilty of treason,' said Marcus Crawford, his massive back towards the man he had once employed.

'No, I would never. You have to believe me, sir,' pleaded the desperate man as he clambered on his knees. 'I could never turn against you.'

Marcus rubbed his forehead, bored with the man's plea of innocence. The cards were stacked against the ex-employee. He had been caught conspiring in a plot that had seen the fall of Marcus's empire and the rise of a rival faction. 'For several years, I've watched my empire grow. And during those years, I've faced my fair share of opposition from competitors, all vying for their place in this business.' Marcus turned to face the man who had betrayed him. 'Out of all of those quarrelling scumbags, not one of them was successful. And do you know why? Because I always trumped over and above them. I did what others refused to do. I did the unthinkable. I was ruthless. And look where that has got me today. I am the boss of my very own mafia. The owner of this grand establishment. All of this because of me and my vision. I succeeded because I took control. When I led, others followed. My men were loyal. That has been the key to my victory.'

From his position of supplication, the pleading man watched Marcus Crawford round the glossy table between them. The big man came to a stop a few feet in front of him.

'Now, the crime you have committed is a first. In all my years I've never had a single man betray me. The thought wouldn't dare cross their minds. But you, you took it a step further. You planned and plotted against me,' said Marcus, driving a meaty fist into his former employee's jaw. The man reeled back, spitting blood onto the laminated floor. 'Did you forget who I am?'

Lying in his bloody mess, his head spinning, the man struggled to utter an audible response. Spectating in silence, Marcus's loyal henchmen watched their boss unleash a hail of blows on the man who had once stood alongside them. Had he not conspired to overthrow the boss, he would not be in his wretched position. He would not have had to suffer the brutal consequences of his duplicitous actions.

Satisfied with his vent of savage rage, Marcus placed the heel of his shoe on top of the man's limp body, his weight threatening to crush the man's ribcage. 'Take this treacherous scum to the pit and bury him. And someone get this mess cleaned up.'

Without hesitation, his henchmen approached the broken man, took him by the arms and dragged him out of the office.

Reaching into his breast pocket, Marcus withdrew a silk handkerchief and wiped the blood off his burly hands. 'Do you have anything else for me, Travis?'

Marcus Crawford's right-hand man, a slim, athletic-looking man, stepped forward. With a reputation for unwavering loyalty, Travis had worked his way up the murky food chain, showcasing his unmistakable worth to his boss. Being a hard man to please, it was rare that Marcus noticed the individual merits of those beneath him. 'Unfortunately, I do, sir. It's Andy Huang. His debt collection was scheduled thirty-six hours ago, but he hasn't come through. We've attempted contact, but he isn't picking up his phone either. How would you like us to proceed, sir?'

Never forgetting a debt he was owed, Marcus squeezed the handkerchief in his palm. 'I want you to pay him a visit. Remind him of his oath and the consequences for not upholding it.'

Nodding in affirmation, Travis turned on his heel and signalled to two men to follow him. As a handful of his lackeys mopped the pool of blood, Marcus turned the handkerchief over in his hands, still agitated by the man he'd beaten to a pulp. His thoughts then settled on Andy Huang. *You failed once, and I let you live. Maybe I need to do something more drastic. Then you'll learn.*

Those who questioned Marcus Crawford's authority didn't live to tell the tale.

Chapter 7

Sitting by the window looking out over the street, James was lost in deep thought. He didn't know what it was like to live without his father, or rather to know that his father would not be leaving the hospital anytime soon, should he survive his ordeal. As much as he disliked the man, he couldn't bring himself to feel hatred. How could he when he was the only father figure he'd ever known? His mother was a constant in his life, the one who ensured he attended college every day, but even then she was almost as distant as his father. With him out of the equation for now, how would his life differ? Maybe Simon had a point. Maybe this was the event that would change things for the better. Maybe it was some sort of karma, some sort of opening in his life. Much like a new chapter. Maybe he and his mother could start over and move away from all of this. But what about Simon? He was his best friend. He couldn't leave him behind. He wouldn't.

As he pondered deeper, his thoughts shifted back to his father. The images of his badly beaten body flashed before his eyes, as fresh as the day he'd found him in the back garden. Who could do such a thing? To brutally beat a man to within an inch of his life. Had his father crossed someone he shouldn't have? Had he got mixed up in the wrong crowd? What wrong could he have committed to receive such a vicious attack? Thinking back to the day of the incident, he couldn't remember much, aside from the strike that had been inflicted by the hand of his father. After that he had felt numb for the rest of the evening. In spite of that, and all the previous times his father had lashed out at him, he hoped in his heart that his father would make a recovery. He may not have the family he wanted, but he didn't want to see what he did have wither away either.

Whatever it is you've got yourself into, whatever it is you've done wrong, know that I forgive you, Father. Not even you deserve such a harsh judgement. Please come back to us.

Taking a final glance outside, James got up and moved away from the window, heading back to the living room where his mother was. The news of his father's grievous condition hadn't had much effect on her; if anything, it had just made her more despondent.

Halfway across the hallway, James paused at a knock at the front door. He watched his mother push herself off the shabby couch and amble her way over. She slid the bolt off the latch and eased the door open. As soon as she did, she was flung back by the force of the door being shoved open. The door creaked on its hinges as three men in dark suits pushed past and marched into the Huang residence. Seeing his mother scramble to her feet, James froze, dumbfounded by the abrupt intrusion.

'Where is he? Where is Andy Huang,' yelled one of the men. Appearing to be the one calling the shots, he stayed put and signalled to the others to spread out and search the house.

'What the hell do you think you're doing?' shouted James's mother, glaring at the man who had asked the question. 'You can't just barge your way in here and do whatever you want. This is our house, our turf!'

In a flash, the man in charge closed the distance between himself and James's mother, backhanding her down onto the carpeted floor. 'I really don't appreciate your tone. So, I'll ask you one more time. Where is Andy Huang? Where is that coward hiding?'

Enraged to see his mother so disrespected, James lunged forwards and grabbed the man by his shirt collar. 'If you touch my mother again, I'll—'

A fist plunged into his gut, bringing him to his knees. 'You might want to think twice about doing that again, little man,' warned the man in charge, cracking his knuckles. 'Now, I came here with one question. Where is Andy Huang?'

James glowered at the man who had struck him. 'Who are you? And what do you want with my father?'

'Perhaps I didn't make myself clear the first time. I'm the one asking the questions. You're the one answering them,' sneered the man in charge. He brushed his suit jacket aside, revealing a gun concealed on his belt. 'For the last time, where is Andy Huang?'

Not having the faintest idea of what was going on, or of the identity of the men who had forced their way into his home, James fell silent. Who were these guys? What did they want with his father? Were they the ones behind his brutal assault?

'The place is empty,' said one of the goons as he and his partner re-entered the living room.

'He's not here, you bastards!' shouted James's mother, regaining her voice. 'And if you think I'm going to tell you where he is, you can go to hell.'

Outraged with not finding his quarry, the man in charge balled his hands into fists. 'Shoot the bitch!'

Obeying his orders, one of the goons withdrew his concealed firearm and pulled the trigger twice, the bullets ripping through James's mother's torso. Her body fell limp in an instant.

'No! Mum!' screamed James, stumbling across the hallway, his legs buckling beneath him. This couldn't be happening. 'Mum! Please, no ...' He grabbed her hands, shaking them.

'That should send a message to that coward,' said the man in charge, his voice devoid of the slightest emotion. 'We're heading back to the casino. Bring the kid along, I'm sure the boss will find some use for him.'

The two goons seized James by his arms and threw a burlap sack over his head, hauling him away from the house and chucking him into the back seat of their black SUV.

<hr>

Horrified by what he was witnessing, Simon silently thanked the silver ring on his middle finger. Hiding amongst the bushes, he had made his way to James's house shortly after being assailed by some sort of extrasensory perception involving his friend and some unidentified men. He didn't know how or why, but something had alerted him to the situation. It was as though the silver ring had known about the house intrusion and had communicated it in some inexplicable way that transcended time and space.

He didn't understand what had happened, but he was glad he had been there to see a slim man in a dark suit exit the residence, followed by two others who held James by the arms and escorted him out. After placing a bag over his head, they tossed him into the back seat of their SUV and drove off.

Feeling an unbridled rage take hold of him, Simon rubbed the silver ring on his finger and a warmth radiated across his muscles, filling him with an unprecedented power he hadn't felt before.

They have taken your friend. We must pursue them. We must make them suffer.

Hearing the whispering voice within, Simon let the ring's power consume him. As the runes began to glow, the dark purple liquid infiltrated his being, enveloping him in its potent embrace. With his strength, speed and senses enhanced, Simon locked onto his targets. The men who had harmed James would be made to answer for what they had done. They would suffer the consequences of crossing him. Vengeance was coming.

Chapter 8

Sweaty, scared and feeling claustrophobic, James couldn't shake the image of his dying mother from his mind. The sickening images and sounds of the gun being fired and his mother's body going limp played on a loop in his mind. He had felt powerless watching her die, watching her life fade away. A pang of guilt stabbed at him. Why hadn't he acted sooner? If he had done something – anything – she might not have lost her life. If he had acted differently, things wouldn't be the way they were. With his mother gone, all he had left was his father: a broken man whose life would undoubtedly be different; that's if he survived his major injuries. His life was on a downward trajectory, and he was helpless to do anything about it. Tears streamed down his sullen face. Where was Simon when he needed him?

The discordant murmuring of voices brought him back to the present moment. He tilted his head in an effort to grasp what was being said. With the sack still over his head, he was blind and oblivious to his surroundings. All he could feel was a vice-like grip constraining his arms. Casting his mind back, he recalled the man who ordered his mother's death saying something about a casino, but he had no idea as to what or where.

Without warning, there was a violent tug and the sack was yanked off his head. Disorientated by the sudden move, James squinted, his eyes sensitive to the bright lights that adorned the room. In front of him, sitting at a glossy desk, he could make out a burly-looking man in a pinstriped suit.

'Well, what do we have here?' asked the big man in a gruff voice. 'None other than the coward's son. You should be glad to know that you don't look like him.'

His eyes now adjusted to the environment, James fixed the man with a vacant stare, his emotions in turmoil.

'The name's Marcus Crawford. In case you haven't figured it out already, I knew your father, Andy,' said the man in the pinstriped suit. 'He used to work for me a number of years ago, long before you were born. He was a delivery man of sorts, selling contraband on the black market. After years of working, he came to me one day, telling me he wanted out. Seeing that he still had a number of jobs left on his tab, I offered to cut him a deal. He was to pay me compensation for the jobs he didn't finish, even if that meant for the rest of his life. Being the cowardly fool he was, he tried to escape, thinking he could evade my sight. As punishment, I had him beaten and thrown in a pit. I made him swear an oath that he'd pay me my compensation money, whether he could afford it or not. Since that day, he has never failed to make the stipulated payments, until recently that is. I have now been informed that he suffered a vicious attack and has been hospitalised. It's too bad, really, as I wouldn't have minded putting him there myself.'

James stared at the man with a pained look, clenching and unclenching his fists.

His face twisting into a sinister smile, Marcus Crawford continued. 'With all of that out of the way, we can now come to your part in all of this. As your father is in no condition to pay his debts, I've appointed you to replace him for the time being. Needless to say, you work for me now.'

Downhearted and dispirited, James fixed his gaze on the laminated floor. He felt empty, devoid of vitality for life. Here he was, helpless again, as he had been throughout his life. Alone, weak and desperate. *What am I to do?*

'You'll be briefed on your first job when the time comes. Until then, get out of my sight,' said Marcus.

The men in suits tightened their grip on James's arms and began to walk him towards the doors. It was then that the double doors burst open and another lackey in a dark suit rushed in.

'Mr Crawford, the casino is under attack!' shouted the distressed man. 'We don't know by who, but we suspect that it must be one of your competitors. They've already laid waste to a dozen or so men and are heading this way.'

Not known to surrender when the going gets tough, Marcus Crawford leapt to his feet. 'Who dares step into my establishment to declare war on me?' he said with a grimace. 'Get the situation under control. Pronto! If it's a war they want, it's a war they'll get.'

Throwing James to one side, the men in suits fled from the office and sealed the double doors shut.

Scarcely aware of the lurking danger, James crawled to the corner of the office and brought his knees up to his chin.

'If I find out you had anything to do with this, there will be hell to pay,' growled Marcus Crawford, glaring at James.

Turning ashen, James closed his eyes, attempting to shut his mind off from the horrors of the world. He wished for respite. He wished none of it were real.

Chapter 9

With caution, Travis McNeil signalled his men to round the corner of the hallway. Unsure of what lay ahead, he peeked around the corner, his pistol at the ready. On seeing the carnage spread out before him, Travis's stomach lurched and bile rose into his throat. The casino's once impeccable hallway was now the scene of a grisly murder. The lifeless bodies of the men Travis had spoken with only earlier in the day now lay still, their blood freshly caked on the white walls and dark carpets underfoot. Deep cuts inflicted on their abdomens revealed their eviscerated entrails, which were spilling onto the floor. Each man was surrounded by a pool of his own blood, if not the next man's. It was a savage butchery, something that Travis had never come across in his criminal career.

'What the hell? Who could have done this?' asked one of Travis's men, his troubled tone betraying his tough appearance.

'I don't know, but we'd better get back to the office,' replied Travis, retracing his footsteps.

As he turned, he felt an uncomfortable sensation of being watched. Stalked. Tilting his head up to the ceiling, he let out a strangled cry. Up above, an immense, dark humanoid creature was glowering back at him, a bloodthirsty hunger in its great, luminous eyes. As his legs buckled beneath him, Travis raised his pistol to the ceiling, opening fire on the alien-like creature.

Alerted to the impending danger, the men in dark suits instinctively turned and opened fire at the humanoid on the ceiling, creating a cacophony of sound. But their bullets did little to deter the creature, simply ricocheting off its smooth, metallic skin. Within the blink of an eye, the creature dropped to the floor, landing on its long, muscular legs. In a flurry of speed and unconceivable agility, the humanoid creature transformed its limbs into razor-sharp weapons, slicing through the men in suits like a hot knife through butter.

Seeing his men fall like flies, Travis discharged his pistol clip and turned on his heel, running for the boss's office, the screams of his dying men filling his ears. Before he could make it to the doors, the crack of a whip filled the air and a rope-like material snapped around his ankle, wrenching him off his feet and pulling him back into the violent fray.

Travis screamed, his bloodied nails grasping at the floor, all too aware of his gruesome fate.

CHAPTER 10

With a mighty swing, Simon brought down his mace-like hand on the screaming man in the dark suit, splattering fresh blood onto the already desecrated walls. With the last man out of his way, he could proceed to the remaining room up ahead. Glancing back at the bloodbath in his wake, he felt the silver ring's power surge through his veins, spiking his adrenaline. As he marched towards the double doors, a ripple of anticipation flickered through his muscles; he felt invincible. If James had been harmed in any way, he would massacre those who were responsible.

There would be no escape from his wrath. Not today, not ever.

Curling his fingers into steel fists, he struck the wooden double doors standing in front of him, bursting them off their once solid hinges. The splintered doors flew across the room, forming a broken heap on the laminate floor. Taking a cautious step into the brightly lit office, he threw furtive glances around, searching for his quarry. To his surprise and dismay, the office was empty, not a single soul in sight. *They were here. We can sense them.* His metallic skin bristled and illuminated briefly. James had been here, along with someone else. It was the person who had taken him. They had been here recently. *Where could they have gone?*

He scanned the room, and his gaze settled on the window behind the desk. No, they couldn't have escaped that way; the window was closed. Even if it had been used, they most likely wouldn't have survived the drop or made it out in time. Casting his gaze elsewhere, he advanced further into the room, drawing in the scent of its former inhabitants. Perhaps—

Outside, the distinct sound of approaching sirens broke through his thoughts. Someone must have heard the gunshots and notified the police.

Best we leave now, lest we attract their attention, whispered the voice deep within. *We will find your friend; we will bring him back. They shall not evade us.*

Heeding the words that emanated from deep within him, Simon shot a final glance around the room, before slinking into the shadows and vanishing from the site.

CHAPTER 11

Concealed deep within the shadows, Simon watched the incoming police cars screech to a halt outside the Grand Casino in Piccadilly; the drivers unaware of the fact that their vehicles were double-parked. It was a sign that indicated how fast the situation had escalated since the first officers had arrived on the scene. Once they had discovered the bodies and the weapons the scene was bound to put the police and the capital on high alert. The amount of security and uniforms that were roaming around the building attested to that. It was a gruesome scene inside the building; he didn't doubt that. But it was also not without its justification. The criminals who had once occupied the casino had committed a number of atrocities in their lifetimes, some much worse than his. He had simply exacted retribution: a poetic justice that saw the guilty answer for their crimes. He wasn't the aggressor here and they the victims. They couldn't be. They had deserved what had come to them, especially for the abduction of James. They had wreaked havoc on his friend's already fragile life and would suffer dearly for it. They had had their chance to walk away but not taken it when the opportunity arose. They had brought this upon themselves and would continue to do so until he eventually found James. By taking his friend, they had all but sealed their own fates.

Turning and walking away from the flashing blue lights of the police cars and the neon lights of the Grand Casino, Simon kept to the shadows, the newly fallen night sky adding to his cloaked cover. His thoughts drifted back to his first target, James's father, and the events following that night. Were they connected in some way? James had been abducted only days after his father's hospitalisation. Was there a link between his father and the men at the casino? Knowing little about the deplorable man in question, it was difficult to draw a connection, but it didn't seem unreasonable. He cast his mind back to the house intrusion and the following kidnapping hours earlier. The men in dark suits had seemed focused and professional, knowing what they had come for. Aside from James, it didn't appear that they hadn't taken anything else from the residence, and judging by the signs, it wasn't a robbery or a random event. It must have been pre-planned. Although the original plan mustn't have involved his friend or his mother. It couldn't have. Why would these men go to all this trouble to abduct a poor seventeen-year-old? It didn't add up. His thoughts flickered back to James's father. There was only one way to clear things up.

It was time to pay James's father a visit.

CHAPTER 12

U nnerved and infuriated, Marcus Crawford glowered out the window of his new, makeshift office, the pitch-black sky and blustery weather a reflection of his mood. He still couldn't comprehend his brush with death only a few hours earlier. As much as he hated to admit it, he had been lucky to escape through his secret passageway, which had spared him from the malicious grasp of his belligerent enemies. Following the escape route through the building and out to a hidden back door, he had taken the boy with him at gunpoint; he would serve as a decoy or hostage, whichever came first. To his relief, it hadn't come to that. In a twist of fate, Marcus's five remaining men had found him first and driven him to his warehouse on the outskirts of Enfield. Since becoming the boss, he had never had to contemplate his own safety. But someone was out for blood and had him fixed in their sights.

Who would dare to attempt such a bold act, storming into his establishment, breaking into his property, looking to kill him? A multitude of possibilities raced across his frantic mind. Was it the East End Mob? Were they trying to dethrone him? Could it have been the South Adams Gang who had tried to rush him? Or maybe it was the Chapel Gang from up north? Whoever it was, whoever was responsible for the brutal murders of his men, they had certainly made a bold statement: they wanted Marcus out – and for good.

Unsure of who to suspect first from his list of potential rivals, Marcus thought back to his actions over the past few days, his mind sifting through the accumulation of experiences. There was the renegade who had attempted to usurp him, but no, it couldn't be him. He had crushed the insurrection before it had time to permeate like a parasite. Shifting focus, his mind centred on his latest business deals and the faces of those he had last spoken with. *No, it couldn't be one of those affiliates, it is unlike them and they wouldn't dare break our agreement. It couldn't be my competitors either; they don't have the manpower nor the resources to carry out such an attack.* Unable to pinpoint who was responsible for the assault on his former casino, Marcus massaged his temples, trying to calm his frayed nerves.

The Grand Casino he had once so proudly owned was now, for the foreseeable future, under the surveillance and jurisdiction of the Metropolitan Police, and whichever other investigative bodies that were brought into the fray. Sooner or later, the smoggy aftermath would catch up with him, and when it did, he would need the best lawyers to untangle him from the web of mayhem. The mere thought of losing his prized possession raised his blood pressure and reminded him of the debts he was still owed.

In turn, one thought led to another, bringing him to the boy he had abducted, James Huang, and his father, Andy. *That quivering son of a bitch*, thought Marcus, his rage returning in full throttle. It was only after his men had taken the boy that his life had taken an alarming turn. Was it chance, coincidence or something else? Sure, his life had taken gravely hostile turns in the past, but he had always managed to stay on top of it. What he had experienced earlier, however, was unprecedented. The reports he had received from his remaining men, the savagery that they claimed to have seen, it was beyond anything that he had ever experienced in his ascension to power. Marcus balled his brawny hands into tight fists. He would find the person responsible for the attack on his casino. He would enjoy watching them suffer.

Turning his attention back to the present, he focused his mind on the boy he'd held captive. For some odd reason, he had a nagging hunch that the kid had something to do with the assault on his casino, and he would find out what it was.

Stepping away from the large, square window, Marcus hastily made his way down to the cellar.

Chapter 13

James still retched at the foul taste of the gag the men in dark suits had previously shoved into his mouth. Though his stomach churned, at least now he wouldn't have to suffer from its vile taste. Sitting on a small metal stool that grated under his weight, he looked about his surroundings, hoping to see something that would work in his favour. But there was nothing in sight that would aid him in his already failed attempt at an escape. With only one dim bulb dangling from the low ceiling, he couldn't see much anyway. To make matters worse, the cellar was filled with a putrid stench that nearly made him puke. Had he not been conscious of the gag earlier, he might have choked on his own spew.

Angst-ridden, he desperately wished to be free from his predicament, but no matter how he struggled, the cable ties around his wrists remained tight; he wouldn't be going anywhere for the time being. With a futile glance at his surroundings, he resigned himself to his fate, allowing himself to slump back down on the rough metal of the stool. His head spinning and his taste buds bittered, he became lost in his frenzied flow of thoughts, the only available respite from his disturbing reality. *Why me? What wrong have I committed? What have I done to deserve such torment?*

Thinking back to recent events, he remembered all of the pain he had already experienced growing up: where he lived, his abusive father, his distant mother, the bullying he had suffered during secondary school and his alienation at college. He had been blighted throughout his whole life; he was a walking tragedy. And now, at the lowest unimaginable point in his life, would he meet his end in this squalid and indifferent dump? Would his life be disregarded and forgotten? If his father did survive his injuries, would he even remember his only son? The idea of fading out of history frightened him. He didn't want his life to end like this. He was too young, too innocent to be deserving of such a cruel fate.

Shaking the depressing thoughts from his mind, James remembered the one person who had been there for him in his most desperate times of need: his best friend, Simon. He was the one person who he could count on throughout his life, and he had no doubt that he would be contemplating his whereabouts at the present moment. *If only you knew, Simon. If only you knew.*

The familiar sound of a door being unlocked interrupted his thoughts. Returning to the reality surrounding him,

James turned towards the rotating knob on the door to his right. With a final click, the door was eased open and two slim men in dark suits entered the room. James recognised the stony faces of the men who had dragged him into the room and bound him. Following shortly after them was a burly man in a familiar pinstriped suit. James instantly recognised the big man as Marcus Crawford: the man who had pointed the gun in his face, taking him hostage for a second time when he'd tried to escape the building. Forced to walk through a narrow passageway, he'd been met by the men, who had carelessly tossed him into the boot of their getaway vehicle. Antagonised by the memories, James glared at the brawny man.

Standing between his lackeys, Marcus regarded James with a lack of concern. 'I'm going to ask you some questions and you're going to answer, boy,' he barked, his tone full of steely menace.

Feeling nothing but enmity for the man before him, James looked away defiantly, refusing to meet his gaze.

Marcus sneered in derision. 'So, you want to play it that way, do you?' With a tilt of his head, he signalled to one of his lackeys. As though activated on command, one of the men in dark suits approached James and sank his fist sink deep into James's gut. James instantly doubled over with a belch, puking out a stream of spew.

'Doesn't taste too favourable, does it?' said Marcus, taking a step back.

Looking every bit as bilious as he felt, James coughed up the last of his vomit, his mouth dry with a sickly taste. 'Please, no more. I'll do whatever you ask. Just, please … no more.'

Marcus smirked with satisfaction as he stepped forwards once again. 'As you are aware, someone mounted an attack on my property in Piccadilly. Would you happen to know anything about that?'

James paused, his mouth agape. *What? What could I possibly know? How could he suspect me?*

'You'll answer my question, unless you wish to regurgitate more than your last meal,' said Marcus, his face twisted in a scowl.

'I swear … I don't know anything about that,' pleaded James. 'I'm just an ordinary teenager who's been dragged into this mess. I never knew you existed until a few hours ago. What could I possibly know?' Looking up into Marcus's cold and appraising eyes, he could see that his words were being considered by the otherwise merciless man. 'You have to believe me. I didn't even know that you knew my father before you told me.'

Appearing to mull the situation over in his mind, Marcus remained silent for a few moments, a strange faraway look in his eyes. 'Unfortunately, I believe you.' Fixing James with a final glare, Marcus turned on his heel and exited the cellar, his lackeys following close behind.

As the last of the men in dark suits stepped out of the bleak room and shut the iron door, James slumped on the stool with a heavy sigh. *What is going on? Will this torture ever end?*

CHAPTER 14

Bruised and beaten, Andy Huang had been confined to his hospital bed for the past few days. In no condition to stand or perform his usual day-to-day duties, he knew he would not be leaving his temperate hospital quarters for a long time. Having received multiple stitches for his injuries, as well as two plaster casts, he tried to shut his mind away from the anguish of his condition. But with nothing else to do, every waking hour he was faced with the same unbearable pain that gnawed at his conscience, reminding him of the crimes he had committed throughout his turbulent life.

He had never thought it would be him who would end up on a stretcher, but here he was. Since that ill-fated day so many years ago, when he had been at the mercy of Marcus Crawford, he hadn't felt so spineless and fearful. The harrowing events of the night of his vicious assault still plagued him: the pain that had been inflicted so mercilessly on his slender body. Most unforgettable of all, however, were the luminous eyes of the dark humanoid creature; the way it had stalked, hunted and harmed him. He was certain that what he'd seen had been real. Like a phantasmagoria, the dreadful memories haunted his conscience; so much so that he was afraid to fall asleep at night, for fear of seeing the creature once again.

In an attempt to block the recurring thoughts, he turned his attention to his late partner and to the son he had neglected. After being informed by the police of his partner's murder and his son's suspected kidnapping, he had felt pangs of guilt and sorrow for the family he had never truly recognised. When he had first felt the feelings of regret, it had been an unexpected and agonising surprise. He hadn't thought he would react so strongly to the news of his sudden and miserable misfortune. If only he could take back his actions. If only he could get the chance to see his son again.

As the tide of grief passed over him, Andy fixed his gaze on the matte grey wall at the far end of his bed. With his eyes unfocused, he became aware of a second presence nearby.

Scanning the length of his room, he felt a cold chill slither up his spine. A flicker of movement caught his attention. In the far corner, where the light failed to cut through the deep shadow, a distinct figure was contorting itself out of the gloom. Panic-stricken, he pressed himself further into to his pillows as the looming figure rose to its full height, its body finalising in form.

Paralysed with fear, he stared up at the tall, dark humanoid that had put him in hospital, its searing purple eyes boring holes into his once again. It must have returned to finish him off.

Before he could so much as squeal, the menacing humanoid closed in on him in a matter of mere seconds, its sheening hand smothering his mouth.

'Scream and I promise it will be your last,' growled the alien creature.

CHAPTER 15

'What ... what do you want from me?' stammered Andy, his heart palpitating.

'Information that may identify the whereabouts of your son, James,' replied the dark humanoid.

'James? I ... I was told he'd been kidnapped. I don't know where or why.'

'He was only abducted after we put you here,' said the humanoid creature, gesturing to the surrounding room. 'I suspect this is not a coincidence.'

Andy cast his mind back to a few days earlier. 'Before you put me here, I had defaulted on some payments to a powerful and dangerous man,' he said in a low voice. 'His name is Marcus Crawford. He's the boss of a mafia based in Central London.'

'The name's new, but I already know about his casino. I was there.'

Andy's eyes grew larger. 'You mean you were the one behind the Grand Casino massacre that I saw on TV?' The pieces were beginning to fall into place.

'To rescue your son, yes.'

'What? Why? Why does the boy matter to you?'

'It's simple. He doesn't deserve to suffer for your misdeeds,' said the dark humanoid. 'The longer you stall on information, the less time your son may have.'

'OK, OK. The man I told you about, Marcus, he's probably gone into hiding somewhere. Somewhere he feels safe.'

'You're going to have to do better than that. I need something useful, and fast.'

Andy raked through his muddled memory. There must be something of significance, surely.

'If James doesn't make it, it will be on your head,' said the looming humanoid, its purple eyes ablaze.

'Uh, I remember a warehouse that Marcus owned in the borough of Enfield. It was a while ago, but he used to go there whenever things got heated,' said Andy. 'If he still owns it, you might find him there.'

Upon receiving the information, the dark humanoid drew itself back, its focus no longer fixed on him.

'Wait,' cried Andy, still overrun with questions of his own.

The dark creature paused, its back sheening in the glimmer of light.

'That night, when you attacked me. Why didn't you kill me?'

Facing away from Andy, the dark humanoid turned its head halfway towards him. 'If it were up to us, you would be dead already. We spared you, only for the sake of your son.'

CHAPTER 16

I t had taken over five hours for Simon to locate the warehouse, but his persistence and extrasensory navigation had successfully led him to his quarry. It turned out that James's father had remembered correctly, and he had been right about Marcus Crawford wanting to keep a low profile. To a casual observer, the warehouse appeared unoccupied and desolate, but that was just a facade.

Simon had seen the men in dark suits make occasional rounds to two black vans parked out in the loading bay adjacent to the warehouse. On each trip, the men had carried heavy-looking duffel bags, loading them into the back of the vans. Marcus must have plans to relocate. Whatever the motive, he was keen to stop them here and now. They wouldn't get the chance to escape, not this time.

As he stole towards the warehouse, his heightened senses kicked in, enabling him to detect the heat signatures emitting from the building. He detected seven, six of which were likely armed men, including Marcus himself. The seventh, however, emanated from below ground level, the source appearing unarmed and somewhat faint. It had to be James; it was the only plausible explanation.

Keeping as low to the ground as possible, he inched his way towards a fleet of white vans, conscious of keeping out of sight of the windows. With the sunrise emerging on the horizon, his cover of night would soon be lost. His thoughts flicked back to his family; his parents would be worried sick, wondering where on earth he had been for so long. He longed to return to them, but there was no going back. His best friend needed him, and he was the only one who could get him out.

Using the stationary vehicles as cover, he peered at the towering grey warehouse, waiting for the men in dark suits to re-emerge from their den. Within a few moments, his wish was granted; the blue exit door eased open, and the three familiar men appeared. As before, they each carried a duffel bag over to the black vans and stowed them in the back. Once they had finished packing, the men shut the rear doors and huddled together, speaking in hushed voices. Repositioning himself, he could just about make out what they were saying.

'Remember to stick to the plan. The boss needs this to work. Niko, I want you driving the first van. Mr Crawford, Eric, Jack and the kid will be riding with you,' whispered the man in the middle. 'As for you, Rob. You and I will be riding in the second van, following close behind. Understood?'

Nodding in unison, the three men dispersed. Two of them took up their positions by one of the two vans while the third man returned to the warehouse, disappearing back into the den.

Seeing this as his opportunity, Simon steeled himself for what he was about to do. He looked at the silver ring on his finger and felt the replenishing surge of energy course through his veins, the dark purple liquid enveloping him once again. With the advantage of darkness no longer an option, there was no way he could take out one man without alerting the other. Deciding to dispatch his targets as quickly and quietly as possible, he crept towards the closest unsuspecting henchman.

Unaware of the imminent danger creeping up on him, the first man would never know what had struck him.

CHAPTER 17

Hearing the commotion outside, Marcus Crawford went pale with trepidation as he hauled his hostage into his office, slamming the steel door shut behind him. Clutching his sawn-off shotgun in one hand and James in the other, he anxiously awaited his enemy's entrance.

'Don't try anything, kid, or I'll blow a hole in your chest,' he warned, tightening his grip on James's futile squirming. He didn't know what to expect. He could use the kid as a hostage, if not for negotiation. And if that didn't pan out, he would use him as a human shield. He didn't see himself going out just yet, at least not like this. Of that he was adamant.

A sudden thud broke through his thoughts as a series of powerful blows dented his steel door, ramming it off the door frame and onto the tiled floor in a twisted heap. Fixing his gaze on the tall figure in the hallway, Marcus felt his heart quiver in his chest, his mind void of comprehension.

Standing in the doorway, the dark humanoid figure shot a baleful glance in Marcus's direction, its luminous eyes boring into his.

'What ... what in hell—?' stammered Marcus Crawford. Behind the giant figure, the walls of the corridor were caked red with blood. 'What is this? What are you? What have you done to my men?'

Ignoring the burly man's questions, the purple creature strode into the room then paused, its eyes shifting from its prey to the boy who was being held hostage.

Marcus Crawford swiftly pointed his barrelled gun at James's head. 'I don't know what you are or who sent you, but if you take one more step, I swear I'll shoot him.'

'Let him go,' came the booming voice of the purple creature, its smooth skin sheening in the light.

'And if I refuse? What then?'

'I'll kill you,' replied the creature, its bright purple eyes unblinking.

Marcus smiled sarcastically. 'Well, if you'd wanted to kill me, you would have done it already. And for some reason, you haven't. What is it you're after? What could you possibly want from me?' His tremoring fingers betrayed his seemingly calm demeanour. 'Is it this wretched kid? Is this about him? Is it him you came for?'

'Unhand him.'

'You see, that's the problem, you freak. You don't have any leverage!' shouted Marcus, trying to sound confident. 'If you want him, you'll do as I say.'

Enraged at the man's defiance, the alien creature unleashed a blood-curdling bellow that reverberated around the room.

Marcus trembled with fear, his fingers twitching and accidently pulling the trigger of his shotgun. Ripping itself free from the barrel, the bullet found its mark, exploding through James's chest, showering his blood onto the tiled floor. Drenched in the boy's blood, Marcus froze. He hadn't meant to do that. The only thing between him and his demise was now out of his grasp. He looked on helplessly as the boy collapsed to the floor. *Oh God! I've done it now.* Marcus's eyes flicked back to the purple humanoid figure, steeling himself for what he feared would come next.

In a blur, the alien creature closed the gap between Marcus and itself, its eyes burning with a new-found fury. Knocking the gun from his clutches, the creature seized Marcus's shoulders, bringing its face mere inches from his.

Restrained and helpless, he watched the creature growl before it sunk its dagger-like limbs into his abdomen, lacerating his innards. The barbaric agony was unbearable. He wanted to shriek in pain, but not a single sound escaped his lips. It was at this moment, his life flashing before his eyes, that he could relate to those he had damaged, to those he had once condemned to brutal torture. In all his years, he had never felt an inkling of remorse. But in these final moments of life, he came to know his mortality. He finally understood the true meaning of pain, the feeling of paralysing dread, the taste of death as he gulped his last breath.

CHAPTER 18

'You know you can talk to me, Simon,' said his mother, Sarah, as she brought a tray with two cups of tea and a plate of biscuits into the living room. She placed the tray on the glass table, then took a seat in the opposite armchair.

Unusually quiet and not feeling much of an appetite, Simon sat with his head lowered, his thoughts still muddled with the memories of his now deceased friend, James. He and his family had just returned home from the double funeral held at the local cemetery, where he had witnessed the burial. Standing by the open graves of James and James's mother, he had watched mournfully as the simple coffins were slowly lowered into the freshly dug-out earth.

I'm sorry, my friend. I'm so sorry …

There hadn't been many people at the funeral; in fact, he could have counted them on one hand. Of the few faces he had seen, he recognised one as a student he had seen around college. As for the others, he didn't know who they were. And James's father hadn't been present, or at least he hadn't seen him in attendance. He was undoubtedly still in no condition to walk, but there must have been some way for him to still pay his respects in person. But then again, maybe it was better that he didn't. A man like him didn't deserve the opportunity to say goodbye, just as James hadn't deserved his fate.

'Simon, I know how much James meant to you. He was your friend, a good friend,' said Sarah in a calm voice. 'But you can't blame yourself for what happened to him. It wasn't your fault and never will be.'

Hearing his mother's reassuring words, Simon wanted to believe them. He so desperately wanted to believe that they were true. But deep down, he couldn't shake the guilt that had burrowed into the bottom of his heart. If only his family knew of his actions. If only they knew of the things he had done in an effort to save his best friend. 'I know, Mum. I know. I just wish there was something more that I could have done. If only I had been there for him.'

'There wasn't anything that you could have done, son,' said Sarah, taking a sip of her tea. 'No one saw this coming. It was an unforeseen catastrophe that has shocked us all. Those people that took him, that … that took his life. They are the ones responsible for what happened, not you. There wasn't anything that you or we could do for that matter, so you can't take it upon yourself.'

Considering his mother's words, Simon looked up, meeting his mother's gaze. 'Mum, do you think those people deserved what they got? For what they did?'

Taking a deep breath, Sarah sat back in her chair. 'I don't think it's our place to say, Simon. All I can say is that sometimes things happen for a reason. We may not always have the wisdom to know why, but sometimes we just have to trust that there is something bigger and wiser than us at work. Because of that, we also can't harbour ill intent towards people, even those who may be criminals. I know they hurt you by taking James, but you must not allow that to stain your heart. They don't deserve that satisfaction, and James would never want that, not even for one second.'

CHAPTER 19

Standing on the bridge, overlooking the river, Simon peered at his distant reflection. He didn't recognise who he was anymore. All the things he had done, all the things he had felt, all the violence and bloodshed. He wasn't the person he once was, not anymore. His grievous actions attested to that. Such carnage, such baneful savagery. He had never been overcome with such rampant rage. He had never thought himself capable of such unthinkable acts. But there he had been, bearing the silver ring that had enveloped him in an unknown, liquid-like substance that had augmented his physical and mental capabilities. It seemed so surreal, the mere thought of possessing such unimaginable power, yet he had been a living example of such a manifestation. A manifestation of power that had been corrupted. A power that brought him nothing but pain and ruin.

In assuming the force of the silver ring, he had unwittingly become a gross embodiment of that which he once despised. In doing so, he had forsaken his humanity, his self, his soul. Turning the ring over in his hands, seeing the engraved runes, he felt an intense repugnance for it. It had had a major influence in his path of destruction. It had whispered to his mind, to his heart. It had changed him. Had he not seen the ring fall, had he not let his curiosity get the better of him, he wouldn't be where he was today: lost, confused and full of regretful anguish. He wished he had never made that dreadful decision.

All he had wanted was to liberate his friend from his oppression. He had never intended for any of this to happen. He had never known such a fate would befall him. He had never known there would be such a grim turn of events. James's death was his fault, even though his mother had told him otherwise. He was the one who had put James's father in hospital, which had led to the death of James's mother, followed by his abduction and his eventual death. Had he not been so selfish, his best friend might still be alive. He would not have had to attend his funeral last week. Because of his intervention, he had wrought nothing but death and despair. Sure, he may have decapitated one head from the hydra of organised crime, and then some, but at what cost?

For one last time, Simon gazed at the ring that had brought him such pain. As he did, he began to feel its mystical pull once again. Its alluring nature was trying to draw him back in, trying to bring his doubts to the surface.

Why resist? Why turn away? Why relinquish our gifts? You are nothing without us.

It was tempting, the unbridled power at his disposal; but whether it was a blessing or curse, he could bear the burden no longer. Enclosing the silver ring in his palm, he drew his arm back and cast the ring as far as he could throw. Arcing through the air, the ring glinted in the sunlight and splashed into the water, disappearing beneath the calm, dark blue waves.

Chapter 20

Marcus Crawford gasped as his eyes suddenly shot open, the memory of his not-so-distant death still fresh in his mind, as though he was reliving it once again. His chest heaving as he panted, he glanced about himself, his nerves jangling at the mere thought of the pain he had been dealt. He took in his surroundings: he was no longer at the scene of his demise, but rather somewhere else entirely, somewhere he had never set foot before.

Feeling his strength slowly return to his aching body, he pushed himself up into a sitting position, giving himself a panoramic view of the uncharted landscape that loomed around him. Filled with dark and forbidding mountains, volcanic ash and bubbling lava, the barren wasteland was akin to the descriptions of a nightmarish underworld, a place Marcus had never believed existed. As he looked up towards the ominous black sky, a cold shiver crawled up his spine, fixing him to the spot.

What is this place? Where am I? How did I get here?

With each of his deep, laboured breaths, the pungent stench of charred wood and decaying flesh filled his nostrils, pestering his sense of smell. Pinching his nose to stop himself from vomiting, he watched the Stygian fumes rise from the steaming magma, its incandescent glow a sign of its scorching heat.

Marcus forced himself up onto his feet and surveyed the gloomy environment surrounding him. With a furtive look over his shoulder, he took a feeble step forwards then froze as a blood-curdling screech echoed off the steep mountainsides. He wasn't alone. He could feel the unmistakable prickling on the back of his neck. Foreign eyes were watching him – but from where? Spinning on his heel, he turned his head in all directions, his squinted eyes ever vigilant for the slightest detection of movement. Then, from the corner of his eye, he caught sight of something creeping from behind a jagged boulder. But what was it? From its obscure form, he was sure it wasn't human. As he stared at the emerging monstrosity, another appeared, followed by countless more, all converging from their hiding places.

As they slithered nearer, Marcus took a step back and spun round. They were surrounding him; an attack was imminent. He straightened himself, pulling his shoulders back. He may be weak, but he was not about to go down without a fight. Not this time.

As the infernal creatures shuffled ever closer towards him, a deep and resonant voice boomed from nearby. 'Step away from the specimen, for he is mine,' said the mysterious voice.

As soon as the words were uttered, the fiendish creatures stopped dead in their tracks.

Marcus eyed them suspiciously as they began to disperse, walking backwards until they had disappeared behind the boulders from which they had emerged.

Feeling a knot bind itself in his stomach, Marcus turned, his eyes descending on the source of the strange voice. Cloaked under the stark shadow of one of the protruding boulders was a being with bright, fiery red eyes. As it stepped out of the darkness, its eyes dimmed, revealing a robed young man with ginger hair.

'You!' said Marcus, recognising the man standing before him.

'Oh, is that any way to greet an old friend?' said the ginger-haired man with a smirk.

Marcus scoffed. 'You are many things but that.' His voice was harsh and disdainful.

'Uh-uh.' The young man shook his head in disapproval. 'Considering I just saved your hide from the clutches of my inquisitive brethren, I think it best you watch your tone.'

'So why are you here? And where on earth am I?' asked Marcus as he folded his arms over his broad chest.

'I'll answer the latter first. You're not on Earth anymore, human. This is the Abyss, the place of limbo for souls such as yours. You're lucky you're still lingering here, for if you hadn't been, I wouldn't have been able to intervene as I have,' said the ginger-haired man. 'That brings me to the former part of your question. I am here because of our agreement. The one you made when you were alive. Do you remember it?'

As Marcus considered the words of the young man, recollection spread through his mind, the memories flashing before his eyes. 'Yes, of course I remember the deal.'

'Good. Do you remember the terms?'

'Yes, I remember those too. In the event that I died before I was ready, I would be given the option to live again, to exact revenge for my untimely demise.'

'You are a sharp one, Marcus, always have been. That's why I like you,' said the young man with a mischievous grin. 'Now, as per those terms, do you choose to accept my offer? Do you seek revenge?'

Marcus's mind flicked back to the last moments of his life, to the dark purple humanoid that had painfully ended it, robbed him of his former glory. He didn't just want revenge, he wanted destruction. He wanted blood. He wanted death. 'To avenge myself? Yes, I do,' he said, his eyes glittering.

'Then it is done, my old friend. You shall taste the sweetness of revenge,' said the young man as his eyes sparkled with a fiery flame. 'But remember! You have only two hours to conduct your business. Once the time has run out, you will be in my debt. You would be wise to keep that in mind.'

'Yes, yes, I understand. Now, can you tell me who or what was responsible for my death?'

'Yes, I can. But it will cost you one hour of your time. Are you willing to make that transaction?'

Marcus shrugged. 'Yeah, just as long as you tell me the identity of that thing that took my life. I don't care what it costs.'

The young man smiled slyly to himself. 'As you wish, my old friend. Now, come closer, and I shall tell you all you need to know about your quarry.'

Chapter 21

'All right, everyone, that brings us to the end of class, and I'll be seeing you in a week's time. I hope you all have a splendid half-term,' said Mr Mansfield.

By the time his fellow students had packed up their bags and filed out of the classroom, Simon was still throwing on his jacket. Pulling up the zip, he looked up to see his English teacher approaching him.

'How are you holding up, Simon?' asked Arthur.

'OK, I suppose.' He shrugged his shoulders. In truth, he hadn't been. Since the untimely and unexpected death of James, he hadn't been fine at all. He still couldn't forgive himself for what had happened, and likely never would.

'You know, when the college was informed about what had happened, it was news to everyone,' said the teacher. 'I know you and James were close, but you can't beat yourself up over it. None of us saw this coming. Therefore, you can't hold yourself accountable, Simon.'

'I know, sir. It's just … it's still a lot to take in.'

'Initially, it is. But I know you'll be OK. You'll get through this,' said Arthur, nodding. 'Over the break, try to do the things you enjoy. It'll help you feel better.'

Simon managed a melancholic smile. 'I'll try. Thank you, sir.'

After wishing his teacher a nice half-term, Simon stepped out into a bright, warm sun shower. A wave of nostalgia swept over him, reminding him of a similar time when the sun had shone so beautifully in spite of the rain. James would always wait for him after class, and they would walk home together, exchanging their thoughts on the long day. Seeing so many other students in groups and pairs, he couldn't help but feel a cavity in his chest, an absence of the good times, the times when James had been at his side.

Unable to think about anything else, he ambled along the pavement, forcing himself not to drag his feet. Out in public, this was not the time nor the place to brood. As difficult as it was to not mope, he tried to remain focused. He needed to be aware of his surroundings, especially on busy roads like these.

Spotting the red figure at the traffic lights, he stopped at the pedestrian crossing and was gazing aimlessly across the road when wailing sirens broke into his reverie. Turning towards the oncoming vehicles, he spotted saw a red fire engine speeding along the road, the cars and trucks up ahead parting to give way. As the fire engine whizzed past, he couldn't stop himself from conjuring up a what-if scenario. *Could he do anything to help?* Had he kept the silver ring, perhaps he could have instigated a rescue, saved as many lives as he could. Imagining himself playing the hero felt good; it brought him temporary comfort. Considering what he had done already, it would tip the scales in his favour. Maybe it would do him some good.

Unfortunately, that was no longer a possibility. He had made his choice. He had cast the ring away. For him there would be no heroic act, no last-minute salvation. All of that was a distant memory, one that would remain locked in the recesses of his mind. As fast as the thoughts surfaced, they just as quickly fizzled out. He was in no position to help anyone right now. With no good reason to walk the rest of the way home, he turned into the underground station, carefully descending the steps, so as not to slip on the wet stone.

Standing on the platform, he waited patiently, his mind mostly vacant save for his teacher's words. '*Over the break, do the things you enjoy. It'll help you feel better.*' As much as he appreciated the condolences and support from everyone who offered it, it didn't mean very much to him. Nothing was going to change the fact that James was dead, and no amount of consolation would bring him peace of mind. Despite all the speculation, he was the only one who knew what had really happened the day James was killed. He had been there, trying to rescue his friend, only to see his plan fail. The crime boss, Marcus Crawford, was responsible for that, he had pulled the trigger, and in turn he had suffered dearly for it. But had Simon not been there, had he not intervened when he did, would James still be alive today? It was a question he couldn't answer. The power that the silver ring had bestowed upon him, and his following actions, would remain a secret known only to him. No one would ever really uncover the truth behind the demise of Marcus Crawford, not even the police.

At the sound of the oncoming train, its beaming headlights nearing the platform, Simon shook the retrospective thoughts from his mind, desiring only to forget the whole ordeal. Perhaps he would consider his teacher's suggestion, in spite of himself.

After boarding the tube, he flumped into one of the many vacant seats. As the remaining passengers disembarked the train, the voice on the loudspeaker announced the closure of the doors, followed by the all too familiar 'Mind the gap'.

Waiting for the train to start moving, Simon looked about the carriage; it was empty. He noted the time on his watch: fifteen minutes past three. Surely there would be more people on the tube at this point in the afternoon. It wouldn't be long before rush hour kicked in.

As he mulled over the surprisingly empty carriage, the monotone voice on the loudspeaker returned. 'Dear passenger, the doors will not open for the rest of the journey. Please remain seated, and he will be with you shortly.'

Bewildered by the sudden and unexpected announcement, Simon looked about. Did he really just hear what he thought he heard? Surely, he was mistaken. He got up from his seat and looked towards the adjacent carriages to his right and left. But there were no carriages on either side, just pitch-black darkness that stretched for as far as he could see. His heart rose into his throat. What in the world was going on? Was he seeing things? Was this real?

'Dear passenger, the doors will not open for the rest of the journey. Please remain seated, and he will be with you shortly,' repeated the monotone voice on the loudspeaker.

Now certain of what he had heard, Simon spun on his heel and peered out of the tube windows. Once again, all he could see was the same inky darkness, devoid of any light. Staring into the abyss, he could feel his head spin as his hands grew sweaty and his stomach churned with anxiety. Adrenaline coursed through his bloodstream as his flight or fight response kicked in. Faced with such unknown circumstances, what was he to do? Casting a final glance around, he reached into his pocket and pulled out his phone. He jabbed at the power button but much to his distress, the phone wouldn't turn on, no matter how much pressure he applied. The device was unresponsive. 'Damn it!' He slid the phone back into his pocket and reached for his backpack.

'I must warn you that whatever you're about to try, it will be of no use here, Simon Jones,' said a posh, male voice.

Simon looked up and froze as he laid eyes on the source of the voice. Before him stood an older man in a white shirt and leather waistcoat. With dark silky hair, chiselled features and light brown eyes, there was something almost ethereal about him.

'Yes, I know who you are, Simon,' said the old man with a dubious smile. 'I've been looking forward to meeting you for a long time.'

Chapter 22

'Come on over, I won't bite,' said the old man, beckoning to Simon to take the seat opposite him.

'Who are you? And what's going on?' asked Simon as he cautiously approached the mysterious man.

'You can call me Cornelius, and we'll get to your questions in just a moment. Right now, I'd like nothing more than for you to take a seat so we can have a chat.'

Despite his nerves, Simon had the strange feeling that he should do as requested. He didn't trust the older man, but what other option did he have?

'I know what you're thinking,' said the old man, 'that you must be asleep and that all of this is just a dream. I can assure you this is no such thing. No amount of pinching, shouting or bellowing will wake you. This is as real as it gets.'

'Why should I believe you?' said Simon. 'I've had lucid dreams before. What makes this any different?'

The old man regarded the teenager with a faint smile then leaned forward. 'Tell me, Simon, does any of this feel like a lucid dream to you?'

Looking about himself, he considered his surroundings. Cornelius had a point. This didn't have the nuanced feeling that his dreams usually had. There was a sense of presence. It didn't feel conjured up, hazy or fleeting. He felt the rough fabric of his seat beneath his fingers. The old man must be speaking the truth. This was no dream. It couldn't be.

'Ah, there it is,' said the man with a twinkle in his eye. 'The realisation that I am not an illusion and that you are actually here right now. With that out of the way, we can get down to the purpose of our meeting.'

Unsure of what to say or do in response, Simon stared back at the old man with a blank expression, completely bemused.

'So, it still hasn't occurred to you, yet? The reasoning behind this,' said Cornelius as he gestured to the surroundings and the pitch-black darkness outside. 'Perhaps this will jog your memory.' Unfurling a clenched hand, the old man revealed something shiny and circular in his palm. 'Does this ring a bell?'

Simon's heart skipped a beat. Lying in the palm of the old man's hand was the silver ring.

'But how did you get that?' said Simon, shrinking back into his seat. If his memory served him right, he had cast the ring into the river and watched it sink below the calm waters. So how was it in the possession of this strange man?

'How did I get it?' said Cornelius with a chuckle. 'I created it, kid.'

Simon's eyes widened. 'So, who are you really? And what do you want from me?'

'Oh, come now, child. You could never come to understand who I really am.'

'Then what do you want from me?'

'You still don't get it, do you?' said Cornelius with a sigh. 'I understand you were just trying to protect your friend, James, but you don't seem to understand that there are consequences to your actions, no matter how well intentioned. It's a cause and effect.'

'So, what are you saying to me?' said Simon, narrowing his eyes.

'Did you really think you could just toss this ring into the river and walk away from everything that has happened?' said Cornelius, leaning back in his seat. 'Did you really think that no one out there knew what you had done, or why you did it? Did you really think that you could simply separate yourself from the force of this ring?'

As the old man spoke, a sensation of unease crept up Simon's spine and his hands grew sweaty. It was as though another entity was creeping into his mind.

'You see, when you used this ring all those weeks ago, you bonded with its force, becoming one with its power. You tethered yourselves to each other. In fact, your bond was so strong that the essence of this ring still lingers within you. You may have relinquished it, but it hasn't relinquished you.'

As the otherworldly sensation grew within Simon, the familiar whispers rose from deep inside him once again: *Do not resist, for it is us.*

'So, until the ring deems you unworthy, or you happen to die first, it is at its discretion whether the bond is severed,' said Cornelius, holding the ring between his index finger and thumb. 'Until then, the ring belongs to you or, rather, you belong to the ring.'

As the old man got to his feet and approached him with the ring, Simon felt his body seize up, his limbs unable to move. Sinking further back into the seat against his backpack, he shook with resistance. He didn't want anything to do with the silver ring – not anymore.

'You seem like a good kid, so I trust you'll use it responsibly,' said Cornelius as he eased opened Simon's trembling hand and placed the ring in his palm. 'It is special, so do take care of it, Simon.'

Still shaking against the immobilising force, Simon watched helplessly as Cornelius turned and walked towards the train doors.

As the doors slid open, the old man paused then turned back to face him. 'I'll be seeing you around, kid. Just know that the ring's only desire is to protect you, and what you do with it from here on out will affect your final outcome in this world. Remember that, and you'll come to realise your potential.'

With that, the old man stepped off the slow-moving train and disappeared into the blanket of darkness.

CHAPTER 23

Simon awoke in a cold sweat, his heartbeat pumping vigorously. Befuddled between dream and reality, he looked around. *What's going on?* Taking a moment to get his bearings, he rubbed his eyes and took a couple of deep breaths, allowing his senses to feed him input. Seeing a sea of various faces and hearing the high-pitched squeal of steel, he remembered he was on the underground. He didn't remember feeling tired but figured he must have fallen asleep at some point on the journey.

Rubbing his forehead, Simon nestled back into his seat, still troubled by the images in his mind. Who was the mysterious man who called himself Cornelius? Did he really create the silver ring? Was any of it real?

His mind brimming with many questions, he took a deep breath and composed himself. *Stop scaring yourself silly and relax. It was just a dream*, he repeated in his mind.

Managing to silence his turbulent thoughts, he took another deep breath and closed his eyes. As his tension eased, he felt a familiar, warm sensation spreading across his body. *No, it couldn't be.* He glanced at his hand, and his heart lurched. There, glittering on his middle finger, was the silver ring. His mouth agape with horror, he shuddered as the words of the old man replayed in his mind: 'You may have relinquished it, but it hasn't relinquished you.'

CHAPTER 24

'Why won't you just come off,' mumbled Simon as he yanked and pulled on the silver ring, trying his best to slip it off his finger. To his dismay, however, he was having no such luck. The ring was tightly bound, and no matter how much he turned and twisted it, it just wouldn't budge.

Downcast and defeated, he slumped back in his armchair, resigning himself to the words of Cornelius. Since returning from the underground station, he had tried everything he could think of to separate himself from the ring, but it remained fixed and unmoving. No amount of pressure made any difference.

As he gazed at it forlornly, the whispering voice within him rose to the surface: *It is useless to resist us, Simon. Relax and cooperate, for our destiny is intertwined.*

'Oh no it isn't,' said Simon out loud. 'When I cast you into the river, I detached myself from you. I didn't want or need you anymore. Why can't you or the old man understand that?'

You are the one who fails to understand, Simon. You were the one who, of your own volition, accepted not only our bond but also the burden of raw power that came with it.

'OK, maybe I mistakenly did. But surely I can choose whether or not I still want to be a part of this?' he said, thinking out loud once again.

As my creator said: it is not up to you, it is up to us, and we don't want to part with you.

'Then how long do you intend to stay?' demanded Simon. 'When will you leave me be?'

As he waited for an answer from the whispering voice, he felt it dwindle away, its presence fading back into the deepest recesses of his mind.

'Wait!' pleaded Simon. 'I still have so many questions.'

Despite his desperate inquiry, the whispering voice remained dormant, unresponsive to his insistent demands. He wanted to know more, but he wasn't going to get answers right now, no matter how much he pleaded.

Sighing with irritation, Simon pushed his chair away from his desk and was about to make his way to the door when he felt an unnatural shift in his surroundings. A sudden drop in temperature followed by the feeling of a sinister presence looming over him like a large, dark shadow stopped him in his tracks. Sensing the source was to his right, he turned on his heel, his heart pounding. There, glaring back at him from the darkness outside his bedroom window, was the gaunt face of a skeletal fiend.

Chapter 25

As the ghoulish creature glared through the glass, its pitiless, red eyes smouldering with a deep hatred, Simon's heart palpitated, his stomach fluttering with pangs of impending doom. Sure, he had experienced some strange occurrences lately, but this far outweighed the others. Whatever that figure was hovering outside, it was pure evil incarnate. It could only be. Glowering back at him with a dark, skeletal grin, it showed not a shred of mercy that he could detect. *What the heck is that?* He hoped the whispering voice would provide him with a swift answer.

That is a lich, an undead evil so ancient it dates back millennia said the whispering voice as it resurfaced within his mind.

Before Simon could fully comprehend the words, the ghoul's cavernous red eyes blazed as it sprang forward, shattering the glass of his bedroom window. In a quick and sweeping motion, the ghoulish fiend seized Simon by the neckband of his jumper, hauling him off his feet and out into the darkness of the cold night.

As the lich soared through the starry sky, Simon flailed to free himself, desperate to get away from the clutches of the diabolical creature. But no matter how hard he struggled, the lich's grip remained agonisingly firm, its clawed hands scraping against his left shoulder. He cried out in pain. Where was the power of the ring when he needed it? If he needed it ever, he needed it now!

Responding to its bearer's urgent pleas, the ring's inner runes lit up with the familiar vibrant purple, its warmth spreading across Simon's body. Seeing the dark purple liquid envelop his limbs, Simon felt the replenishing surge of energy course through his veins once more, pumping up his adrenaline and enhancing his spatial awareness.

Also noticing the transformation mid-flight, the ghoulish creature unleashed an ear-piercing screech, descending in altitude at the drastic change in weight of its prey. Not giving his fiendish enemy a chance to re-adjust its grip, Simon remoulded his clenched fist into a dagger-like weapon and drove it deep into the lich's neck until he heard the crunching of bone. With that, the ghoulish monstrosity's grip loosened, enabling Simon to kick himself free of the diabolic abomination.

Still at high altitude, Simon plummeted towards the forest below, scratching and tumbling against the many trees and their spindly branches. Falling too fast to slow his descent, he watched as the muddy grounds rushed up to meet him, finally making impact in a large splatter of sludge. As he took a brief moment to pull himself back together, he felt the ring's energy flow through his body, healing his minor wounds, as well as gratitude. What would have happened to him without the ring's intervention? Surely, he would have met a swift end.

As he pulled himself to his feet and flexed his rippling muscles, he looked up to see his fiendish enemy dive down and make a sharp and ungracious landing on one of the mud-caked rocks in front of him. From the advantage of his upright position, he was able to get a better look at the fiend that had attacked him. Draped in dark and tattered robes, the creature had red eyes that flared from its deep and bony eye sockets. The ghoul was a terrifying creature to behold.

'At last, I finally get my chance to make you suffer for what you did to me!' growled the lich as it pointed a clawed finger at Simon. 'You stripped me of all my glory, discarded my achievements, destroyed my empire!'

Surprised by the fiend's sudden outburst, Simon frowned and shook his head. 'What are you talking about? I don't even know who you are.'

'Oh, but you do, Simon,' said the lich in a cruel voice. 'How can you forget when you were the one who looked me in the eye as you took my life? How can you forget when you were a witness to the murder of your pathetic friend?'

Simon tilted his head to one side, his eyes narrowing. *How was it possible?* 'Marcus? But you're dead. How can you be standing before me?'

'You'll find out soon enough, once I've torn out your heart and feasted on your bones,' said the lich with a snarl as it lunged forwards with its claws outspread.

Sensing the attack mere seconds before it was launched, Simon sidestepped, evading the reach of the undead fiend's flurry of wild swipes, and tackled it into the thick trunk of a tree. Bringing his powerful arms up, he clasped his left hand around the lich's neck and speared its torso with his dagger-like appendage. As he twisted his arm further into his enemy's decayed abdomen, crushing whatever innards still remained, a wide grin spread across its skeletal face.

'You can't put me down the same way twice, Simon,' said the lich, yanking Simon's hand from the rotting hole in its body. 'I feel no pain anymore.'

Feeling the fiend's razor-sharp talons stab into his arm, Simon took a swing with his free hand, ramming his massive fist into its emaciated face. Despite the audible crack, the lich shook off the heavy blow, its eyes scorching with a fiery rage. As Simon took another swing at the undead creature, it raised its bony forearm, parrying his quick attack and countering it with a bone-jarring headbutt.

Simon stumbled backwards from the devastating blow, and the lich sprang forward, hoisting Simon off his feet and slamming him down into the muddy earth. As he grovelled in the muck, scrambling to pick himself up, a heavy blow plunged deep into his back, followed by a barrage of slashes and strikes across the length of his body. Shrieking out in pain, he felt his strength wane as his arms shook with fatigue. Barely able to push himself up, he slumped on his hands and knees, too weak to stand and continue the fight.

'I want you to know something, Simon,' said the ghoulish fiend with a sinister grin. 'As much as I've enjoyed causing you such pain, I feel that you haven't suffered nearly as much as you should. Therefore, I want you to think of your family as I go to slaughter them. I want you to remember what you once had, only for it to be stripped away.'

Feeling his blood boil at the mere prospect, Simon tilted his head, fixing his nemesis with a threatening glare.

'It must feel terrible, knowing that you couldn't save your friend, and now you won't be able to save your family,' said the lich as it prepared itself to take off. But rather than leap into the air, the lich suddenly froze in position, its feet remaining fixed to the murky ground below it. 'What's going on? I... I can't move,' shouted the undead fiend as its body squirmed against the invisible force that shackled it. 'This isn't right. I've still got time. I've still got fifteen minutes.'

'Indeed, you do, Marcus. But you forget a crucial detail,' said a deep and resonant voice.

Turning his head towards the direction of the sound, Simon matched the mysterious voice to a face. Approaching from the cover of the trees was a robed young man with ginger hair and, rather curiously, sparkling red eyes.

'You see, Marcus, the deal stipulated that you only take action against those solely responsible for your death. It never stated that you had permission to go after anyone else,' continued the ginger-haired man, coming to a stop in front of the undead ghoul. 'By initiating such an action, you have hereby breached the terms of our agreement.'

'You underhanded son of a bitch! You sold me short of the deal!' shouted the lich, gritting its rotten teeth.

'What can I say. It's my nature. As you have yours, I have mine,' said the ginger-haired man with a smirk. 'You really shouldn't be surprised, Marcus. I thought you would have known better than to place your trust in one such as myself.'

'You smug bastard! I'll kill you for this!' hissed the ghoulish fiend, its red eyes smouldering.

'Oh, we'll see about that,' said the young man as his smirk was replaced with a cold and sullen expression. 'You have no idea of the torment that awaits you.' Lifting a single finger, the young man silenced the lich's wailing before a wall of fire sprung up around them both.

Mesmerised by the flickering flames, Simon's eyes widened with astonishment. What in the world was going on? Who was that ginger-haired man? What deal was he talking about? As the questions raced across his mind, the flames of the fiery wall flashed brilliantly then fizzled out, revealing an empty clearing in the murky waters of the forest floor. The strange ginger-haired man and the undead ghoul where nowhere to be seen.

Simon eased himself up off the ground, the strength finally returning to his battered body. As a fresh, rejuvenating surge of energy coursed its way along his veins, he cast his mind back over the events of the past few days: from the mind-bending train incident to his battle with Marcus's undead spirit. What did it all mean? Did it mean anything at all? Had he brought all of this upon himself? What would his life be like had he not discovered the ring in the first place? Would Cornelius return to answer his many questions?

Simon shrugged. Who knows what the not-so-distant future had in store for him? But whatever it was, he was adamant he would rise to meet it. One thing was clear: he needed the silver ring more than ever; he would not part with it. With it at his disposal, he would be ready to face whatever came next.

Acknowledgments

Books are not one-person endeavours. Creating them and getting them out to readers is a commitment that takes dedication. That's why I am so grateful to my editor, and to all of you who supported and helped make this book possible. I could not have done it without you!

ABOUT THE AUTHOR

Key Dawkins is an inspired, speculative writer from the UK. Since childhood, he's always wanted to write and publish a book. This is his third one within the urban fantasy and thriller genre, and first within the young adult genre.

www.ingramcontent.com/pod-product-compliance
Lightning Source LLC
Chambersburg PA
CBHW021739190726

48288CB00009B/3102